"THE MAN WHO KILLED THE CURE"

A play by

Luke Yankee

"I know the work of Dr. Max Gerson better than just about anyone, and with good reason. He was my grandfather, and I grew up at his dinner table. One of the things that impresses me the most about *The Man Who Killed the Cure* is the way Luke Yankee has taken the story of Dr. Gerson and dramatized it in a way that is entertaining, compelling, yet stays true to the integrity of his pioneering work in the field of natural healing. The play brings Gerson's story to life in a way that will ignite an important and desperately-needed conversation about natural health in all who see it. I applaud this fine piece of writing and I hope it enjoys many productions around the world for years to come!"

Howard Straus – grandson of Max Gerson and author of
"Dr. Max Gerson: Healing the Hopeless"

*For my mentors, Mickey Birnbaum and Joshua Malkin –
who gave me inspiration…and so much more.*

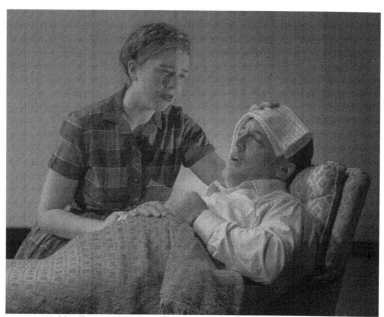

Ashley Rose as Charlotte Gerson and Tom Juarez as Max Gerson
in the original production of *The Man Who Killed the Cure.*

Noah Wagner As Rudolph Heller
in the original production of *The Man Who Killed the Cure.*

(Photo credit: Paul Kennedy)

The Man Who Killed The Cure was first presented at the University of California, Irvine opening on February 25, 2017, directed and produced by Don Hill. The set design was by Keith Bangs; the costume design was by Marcy Froehlich; the lighting design was by Wesley Charles Chew; the sound design was by Leonardo Moradi; the voiceover artist was Robin Buck and the production stage manager was Alex Meyer. The cast was as follows:

Rudolph Heller - **Noah Wagner**

Max Gerson - **Tom Juarez**

Helga/Young Charlotte/Alice Hirsch/Waitress - **Melissa Musial**

Carmichael/Mr. Wienski/Radio Actor/Walter Fleming - **David Sasik**

Long John Nebel/Geroge Grimson/Sign Painter/Eilert Lovborg – **Jordan Kay**

Charlotte Gerson/Gretchen/Mrs. Hammersmith/Hedda Gabler/Anna Hendricks/Attendant/Receptionist - **Ashley Rose**

Special thanks to Max Gerson's grandchildren,
Howard Straus and **Margaret Straus**,
for their encouragement and support.

CAST OF CHARACTERS

(4 men, 2 women*)

Dr. Rudolph Heller - a headstrong German doctor. Warm, charming, egotistical and seemingly unflappable. Ages from mid 30's-mid 60's.

Dr. Max Gerson - also a German doctor. Intense, earnest and totally focused on his work.
Ages from mid 30's-mid 60's.

Helga - Rudy's mistress. Attractive, late 20's, totally devoted to Rudy in a codependent way. Smarter than she thinks she is. (Also plays Young Charlotte, Alice Hirsch, Waitress, Call-Girl and Woman in Coat)

Mr. Carmichael - early 30's, a drug rep for the Riser Pharmaceutical Company. A charming, unscrupulous business-man. (Also plays Mr. Wienski, Radio Actor and Walter Fleming.)

Long John Nebel - early 40's; an affable, radio talk show host (also plays Medical Board Chairman, Eilert Lovborg, Sign Painter and George Grimson).

Charlotte Gerson - Max's daughter, 40's. A straightforward, no-nonsense woman (also plays Gretchen, Mrs. Hammersmith, Hedda Gabler, Anna Hendricks, Attendant and Nurse)

Place: The play takes place in Hamburg, Germany and in New York City from the 1934 to 1949. The epilogue is set in San Diego in the year 2000.

The play is presented on a unit set consisting of different playing areas, with scenes flowing from one area to the next through shifts in lighting in an almost cinematic manner. Each character has one basic, period costume (possibly slightly more for the women) to which they add or subtract a hat, a lab coat, a jacket, etc., to create the feel of an acting ensemble.

*While the play was written to be performed with a cast of six actors, roles can be divided among a larger cast depending upon a theatre's specific needs. It is important, however, that Max and Rudy play only those roles and show a transition in age simply through their physicality and vocal abilities.

SPECIAL NOTE

Anyone receiving permission to produce THE MAN WHO KILLED THE CURE is required to give credit to the Author as sole and exclusive Author of the Play on the title page of all programs distributed in connection with performances of the Play and in all instances in which the title of the Play appears for purposes of advertising, publicizing or otherwise exploiting the Play and/or a production thereof. The name of the Author must appear on a separate line, in which no other name appears, immediately beneath the title and in size of type equal to 50% of the size of the largest, most prominent letter used for the title of the Play. No person, firm or entity may receive credit larger or more prominent than that accorded the Author.

While this play is inspired by actual events, it is not to be considered definitive, healthcare information. If you have an illness, consult with a medical professional. The information presented herein is intended as entertainment and does not presume to be medical advice.

ACT ONE

PROLOGUE.

> *(While the houselights are still up, a plain-looking, middle aged WOMAN enters in a cloth coat and glasses with a scarf on her head. She sits by herself isolated in a spot and waits, patient and content.)*

> *(As the houselights dim, we hear Judy Garland singing "Get Happy" from the film, Summer Stock. Lights up downstage right on the corner of an early 1950's, upscale, living room. There is a comfortable chair with an ottoman, a small table and a coat rack.)*

RECORD

"Forget your troubles, c'mon get happy,
We're gonna chase all your cares away.
Shout Hallelujah, c'mon get happy,
Get ready for the judgment day."*

> *(A well-to-do man in an expensive suit enters, crosses to the hi-fi and scratches the record violently as he switches it off. His name is RUDOLPH HELLER. His public persona is calm and unflappable. When he addresses the audience, he is intense and easily agitated.)*

---

* Rights to perform this play do not include rights to the use of this song, which must be obtained directly from ASCAP music licensing at http://www.ascap.com.

RUDY
(to audience)

We buried Max Gerson today. He was one of the most important men in the history of medicine...and you've never heard of him. He was a genius, a scholar, a healer and my best friend for thirty years.

After we'd stopped working together, we still met at the same café twice a week. The waitress would chase others away. "No, you can't sit there! That's Doctor Heller's table!" We'd sit for hours talking about our patients, our lives back in Hamburg. Neither of us ever felt like this was home. He wanted to die in Germany, but by then he was too sick to travel.

(Rudy pours himself a drink.)

Max did it, you see. He did what everyone said couldn't be done. He solved one of the great mysteries of the modern world. And I made sure it was buried with him.

Perhaps the worst part is that he knew. Possibly all along. And yet this man had such grace, he never said a word. I was his Judas, his Lucretia Borgia, his Brutus. He let me bugger the life right out of him until there was nothing left. He died penniless, in debt up to his neck with nothing to show for it. All because he had something to prove. And yet, as he was hanging onto life by the tiniest thread, there was more brilliance in this one man than you or I could ever hope to know in twenty lifetimes. *(Rudy makes the sign of the cross.)* God rest your soul, Max Gerson. You fucking idiot!

SCENE ONE.

(The Woman in the Coat exits. Crossfade to the examining room of a medical clinic in Hamburg, Germany. The humble office is clean but sparse. There are two entrances:

one leading outside and one leading to the
rest of the flat.)

(DR. MAX GERSON, a man in his   thirties,
examines some dirt under a   microscope. He
is focused, driven and idealistic. Max
examines the dish of earth as a thirty-
something Rudy enters carrying an empty
valise.)

RUDY

You haven't started packing?

MAX

Rudy, you have to see this!

RUDY

Max...

MAX

Just look.

(Picking his battles, Rudy puts down the valise
and crosses to the microscope. Max is like a
little boy with a new toy.)

MAX (cont'd)

Tell me what you see?

RUDY

I see a bunch of organisms moving away from the soil.

MAX

That's because it's one of those new, synthetic fertilizers. They can't
stand the chemicals so they move as far away from it as they can.
Now, in this one, with real dirt, they stay put...

(Max reaches for another dish as Rudy stops
him.)

RUDY

You do realize we're leaving in two hours?

> *(GRETCHEN, Max's pleasant-looking wife,
> and YOUNG CHARLOTTE, Max's young
> daughter, enter.)*

GRETCHEN

You haven't started packing?

> *(Rudy and Gretchen exchange a look. Max
> returns to his microscope.)*

RUDY

I'll help him, Gretchen.

YOUNG CHARLOTTE

Vati, why are you looking at dirt?

> *(Max stays focused on the microscope. Rudy
> takes Young Charlotte and puts her on his
> lap.)*

RUDY

Because he's trying to grow you a baby brother for your sixth
birthday!

YOUNG CHARLOTTE

That's not how babies are born, silly!

RUDY

No?

YOUNG CHARLOTTE

No! You cut the cabbage and the baby pops out!

RUDY

Lottie, you're getting so smart!

*Rudy kisses Young Charlotte on the
forehead..)*

GRETCHEN
Mr. Wienski called. He'll be thirty minutes late.

RUDY
(to Max)
You don't have time to see any more patients!

MAX
This is the last one.

RUDY
What if he's a spy for the SS?

MAX
He has migraines!

GRETCHEN
Rudy has a point, *liebchen*. We can't trust people the way we used
to.

MAX
I don't know how to act any other way.

(Gretchen kisses Max tenderly.)

RUDY
Max, you've got to start packing!

MAX
I can't touch the office until after I see Mr. Wienski.

RUDY
(sighing)
I'll start with your clothes.

MAX

Don't forget my tan sweater.

RUDY
(sarcastically)

Yes, dear.

RUDY (cont'd)
(to audience)

As Max examined his last patient, I packed for him as fast as I could. Whenever he was under stress, he poured himself more deeply into his work. It drove me mad. I could only imagine how Gretchen must have felt.

(Lighting transition to show a passage of time. As Max is examining MR. WIENSKI, a man with a bad skin rash, Rudy is scooping up files and equipment and putting them into a valise as fast as he can.)

MAX

Now, Mr. Wienski, I want you to try eating nothing but fresh apples for the next week.

MR. WIENSKI

Apples? What will that do?

MAX

I've been experimenting with the effect of nutrition on the body. It took away my migraines. It might do the same for you.

MR. WIENSKI

Where do I get them?

MAX

Try Steiner's. If anyone will still have fresh produce--

MR. WIENSKI

It closed last week. Forced out of business by the Nazis. They took Mr. Steiner away.

MAX

That's right. Then try Brodowski's.

(Rudy enters and grabs more files off the desk.)

MR. WIENSKI

Brodowski's prices have tripled. I haven't got enough rations.

MAX

Here. Take mine.

(Max reaches in his desk and hands him a ration book. Mr. Wienski looks like he just won the lottery.)

MR. WIENSKI

Thank you, Dr. Gerson! Now I can feed my family!

(He throws his arms around Max, hugging him tightly. Max freezes, then gently pulls away.)

RUDY

Max! We have to go.

MAX

Good bye, Mr. Wienski.

MR. WIENSKI

God bless you, sir. I wish I could pay you, but I gave your wife two loaves of my homemade pumpernickel. *(Whispers)* For your journey. *(To Rudy)* Good night, Dr. Hellerbach.

(As Mr. Wienski exits, Rudy thrusts a half-packed suitcase into Max's hand.)

RUDY

They could be here any minute. Hurry!

(Max starts packing.)

RUDY (cont'd)

I wish you hadn't given him all of your rations. We might have needed them to bribe a soldier.

MAX
(calling)

Gretchen! Don't forget Lottie's doll!

RUDY

Shh! I sent them on ahead. They'll meet us near the train station.

MAX

Why? We shouldn't be separated now.

RUDY

It will take them longer. Lottie is too big to carry. And we mustn't walk together. The four of us could look suspicious.

MAX

You know, you don't have to go. This is about the Jews.

RUDY

Today the Jews. Tomorrow, who knows?

MAX

Rudy, you know that's not true.

RUDY

You think I'd let you go without me? It's been illegal for Jews to practice medicine for more than a year. We're foolish to have let it go this long. We've got to get you someplace safe.

(Max dumps his suitcase onto the floor and starts   sorting through everything.)

RUDY (cont'd)

What are you doing?

MAX

I have to make sure you packed my blue cashmere socks.

RUDY

What?!

MAX

They were a wedding present from Gretchen! She knitted them herself.

RUDY

Max! She can knit you another pair in New York!

(Rudy grabs Max and forces him to take several deep breaths. He stuffs the contents back into Max's suitcase.)

RUDY (cont'd)

You have the passports?

MAX

Yes.

RUDY

And the transit papers?

MAX

Yes, it's all here. How did you--?

RUDY

Don't ask. And don't ask me again how much they cost.

                          MAX

I'll make it up to you someday.

                          RUDY

A fresh start in America will help us both. And I'm not ready to
break in a new partner.

                          MAX

And you'd miss me. You know you would.

                          RUDY
                       (warmly)

Shut up.

                              *(There is an intense pounding on the front
                              door.)*

                          MAX

The kitchen! Quickly!

                              *(Rudy and Max bolt through the house as the
                              pounding gets louder and more insistent.)*

                              *(Lights transition to a spotlight downstage.
                              Rudy steps into it and addresses the
                              audience.)*

SCENE TWO.

                          RUDY

As we approached the train station, we caught up with Gretchen and
Charlotte. Three different times we had to duck into alleys to hide
from the soldiers. Thank God there was no moon that night. Finally,
just as we were running the last fifty meters, Gretchen got her foot
caught between two cobblestones.

                              *(Gretchen struggles to free herself. Young
                              Charlotte keeps running.)*

GRETCHEN

Lottie!

(Young Charlotte stops and stares at her mother, unsure what she should do. Max re-enters and quickly drags her offstage.)

RUDY

She was so loaded down with suitcases and parcels, she couldn't move. As Gretchen bent down to take off her shoe, something fell out of her pocket: a necklace with a star of David. A Nazi soldier spotted it. He commanded her to stop. In a panic, she ran. The next thing I knew, gunfire rang out. The soldier had shot Gretchen in the back. I can still see the blood spattering against her leather valise.

(Young Charlotte runs onstage and screams.)

YOUNG CHARLOTTE

Muti! Noooo!

(Young Charlotte tries to run to her mother. Rudy stops her as Max enters.)

MAX

Gretchen! Gretchen!

(Max screams and cries and starts to run to her. Rudy grabs him and puts his hand over his mouth. Every time he removes it, Max WAILS. Young Charlotte stands next to Max, shaking in stunned silence.)

RUDY

Max, listen to me. We have to get on that train. There is nothing you can do for Gretchen now. For the sake of all of us, especially your daughter, we must walk out of here calmly. Do you understand?

Max's

*(Max nods. Rudy removes his hand from
mouth.)*

RUDY (cont'd)

Lottie, you must be quiet as a mouse until we get onto the train.
Alright?

*(Young Charlotte turns upstage as if she is
vomiting.)*

RUDY (cont'd)

Max, help her.

*(Max puts his arm around Young Charlotte.
Rudy, Max and Charlotte cross the stage in
stunned silence. Pause.)*

*(The shrill sound of a train whistle melds with
the low moan of a boat whistle.)*

RUDY (cont'd)

The voyage was terrible. The seas were rough and Max hardly left
the cabin. Charlotte was seasick most of the time. That's when the
pain began in her leg. I thought we'd never make it to New York.

SCENE THREE.

*(A cramped, ships cabin. Max applies a cold
cloth to Charlotte's forehead as she lies in
bed. Rudy enters.)*

RUDY

Are you ready?

MAX

I can't leave her.

RUDY

No better?

(Max shakes his head. Rudy crosses to Young Charlotte.)

RUDY (cont'd)

Hello, Lottie.

YOUNG CHARLOTTE

Only *Muti* calls me that!

RUDY

But, I've always called you--

YOUNG CHARLOTTE

Not any more.

RUDY

I understand. Charlotte, may I look at your leg?

(Charlotte pulls back the blanket. He examines her for a moment. Rudy tries to hide how alarmed he is by what he sees.)

MAX

You go on to dinner.

RUDY

I'll bring you both some stew.

MAX

Vegetable broth.

RUDY

Beef stew would make her stronger.

MAX
(sharply)

Vegetable broth. Thank you.

(Rudy motions for Max to step outside with him. They cross downstage.)

RUDY

It looks like bone tuberculosis.

MAX

Impossible.

RUDY

Why?

MAX

Because I'm not losing her, too.

RUDY

Max, I know how you feel, but you must face the fact that--

MAX

No!

RUDY

Bone tuberculosis is fatal.

MAX

If that's what she has, I'll heal her.

RUDY

You're being ridiculous! She should be in the ship's hospital where she would get--

MAX

I'll <u>heal</u> her, Rudy!

RUDY

Suit yourself. *(to audience)* Finally, we arrived in New York Harbor. Was this really the land of opportunity? It had to be better than what we'd left behind. If Max and I had any idea...

SCENE FOUR.

>   *(Lighting transition. Ocean sounds and*
>   *passengers are heard. Rudy crosses*
>   *downstage, followed by Max and Young*
>   *Charlotte, who holds a crutch. They are all*
>   *focused downstage. The other actors mill*
>   *about as passengers.)*

RUDY

I must say, she's even more impressive than I thought she'd be.

>   *(Max puts his arm around Young Charlotte.)*

MAX

Look, Charlotte! That's Lady Liberty!

YOUNG CHARLOTTE

Why does she have spikes on her head?

MAX

It's a crown.

YOUNG CHARLOTTE

It looks like the spike the German officer had on his hat when he shot *Muti*!

MAX

It's not like that at all, *liebchen*.

YOUNG CHARLOTTE

I don't want to go!

29

MAX

You'll love it here.

YOUNG CHARLOTTE
(hysterical)
No! They're going to kill you the way they killed *Muti*!

RUDY

Max, maybe you should take her back to the cabin until we're ready to disembark.

MAX

Yes, perhaps you're right. Come darling.

YOUNG CHARLOTTE

No! I don't want to go to America! Nooo!

> *(Max exits with Young Charlotte screaming and crying.)*

RUDY
(to audience)
Poor little thing. She must have known on some level she was going to die. And Max was in total denial, still saying he was going to heal her. Who did he think he was? I felt sorry for them both. We found apartments near each other, finally procured our American medical licenses and rented an office we could share.

SCENE FIVE.

> *(Lights up on Max and Rudy as they enter an empty office with a few boxes. Max hesitates.)*

RUDY

Shall I carry you over the threshold?

> *(Max laughs.)*

MAX

Not as much space as we had in Hamburg, but it'll do.

(Rudy peruses the space.)

RUDY

The reception area is larger. People won't mind waiting so long.

MAX

There's not much room for my plants.

RUDY

You can put a fern on your desk.

MAX

I meant my specimens. For my research.

RUDY
(sternly)
Max, we're making a new start!

MAX

You saw the results I had in Hamburg.

RUDY

In a few freak cases.

MAX

Remember Mr. Wienski? The day we left Hamburg?

RUDY

Of course.

MAX

I put him on a diet of nothing but apples. His migraines went away in a week. He stayed on it and his skin tuberculosis cleared up.

                              RUDY
And you think it was the oranges?

                              MAX
Apples.

                              RUDY
Whatever. Tell me you haven't said this to anyone else.

                              MAX
Not yet. But once I start treating people --

                              RUDY
Max, no.

                              MAX
Why not?

                              RUDY
There is nothing in the literature of legitimate experimentation to
suggest that nutrition has any effect on disease. A tumor is a tumor.

                              MAX
What if I can prove it?

                              RUDY
Max, you've been under a lot of pressure lately. The stress of the
move and --

                              MAX
I can, Rudy.

                              RUDY
We need people to take our practice seriously. Treating people with
apples?

                    *(Laughing to himself, Rudy exits with a full
                    wastepaper basket, empties it and re-enters.)*

32

MAX

You don't have to insult me.

RUDY

How did I--?

MAX

You think I'm a quack, don't you?

RUDY
(patiently)
I think you're over-reacting and could get us into trouble.

MAX

You don't understand American culture, do you?

RUDY

I don't...?

MAX

It's not about any sense of community here. All anyone cares about is themselves.

RUDY

I thought you wanted to succeed here.

MAX

Of course I do.

RUDY

Then stop being such a pessimist. We're not under Hitler's thumb anymore.

MAX

Sometimes I wonder if it's really all that different.

RUDY

Are you hearing yourself?

MAX

I'm on to something, Rudy! Possibly something big. And you won't
even let me try it?

RUDY

I'm sorry, Max. Natural healing feels unethical to me.

MAX

Then perhaps we should keep our patients separate.

RUDY

You're <u>that</u> determined to do this work?

(Max takes a framed photo of himself,
Gretchen and Young Charlotte and places it
on one of the boxes.)

MAX

It helps me to forget.

(Rudy nods.)

MAX (cont'd)

Charlotte still has nightmares.

RUDY

What about you?

(Pause. Max stares at Rudy intently, fighting
back tears.)

MAX

Why didn't you let me say goodbye?

RUDY

What?

MAX

He shot her like a dog in the middle of the street! Why didn't you let
me go to her?

RUDY

And get us all killed? Please explain to me how that would have
helped the situation.

MAX

No proper burial. No rabbi.

RUDY

Is that what you want? A funeral for Gretchen?

(Max nods.)

RUDY (cont'd)

Alright. Find a rabbi. Say the Kaddish.

MAX

It would give me peace of mind.

RUDY

Whatever it takes to make you stop blaming me.

MAX

I'm sorry. I didn't mean it that way. You have no idea how hard it is
to be a single parent. Sometimes I think the Nazis shot the wrong
one.

RUDY

Now you're being ridiculous.

(There is a KNOCK at the door.)

RUDY (cont'd)

I have a surprise for you.

> *(Rudy crosses to the door. A moment later, he enters followed by a humorless SIGN PAINTER in his forties with his box of paints.)*

RUDY (cont'd)

Max, I'd like you to meet--

MAX

Ernst Eberstadt?!

SIGN PAINTER

You know me?

MAX

I saw your last show in Berlin at the Academy of Arts. You're brilliant!

SIGN PAINTER

Thank you. Shall I get started?

> *(Max looks confused.)*

RUDY

Herr Eberstadt is here to paint our names on the door.

MAX
(shocked)

But, that would be an insult!

SIGN PAINTER

In Berlin, it would have been an insult. Here, I need the work.

RUDY

Thank you, Herr Eberstadt. I want to help however I can.

MAX

It's a great honor to meet you, sir.

(The Sign Painter consults a notepad.)

SIGN PAINTER

So, you want it to read Dr. Max Gerson and Dr. Rudolph
Hellerbach?

RUDY

Actually, I'm changing it. To Heller.

(The Sign Painter nods and exits.)

MAX

Why would you want to do that?

RUDY

Hellerbach sounds so...

MAX

German?

RUDY

We can't help the times we live in, Max.

MAX

I don't see how that will make any difference.

RUDY
(laughing)
Never lose your naiveté, my friend. It's part of your charm.

SCENE SIX.

> *(Crossfade to a handsome RADIO ACTOR in
> his thirties. He stands in front of a
> microphone holding a cigarette as he*

*addresses the audience, speaking with great
authority and charm.)*

ACTOR

If you were to follow a busy doctor making his daily rounds, you'd
have a pretty tough time keeping up with him. Time out for many
men of medicine usually means just long enough to enjoy a good
smoke. And since they know what a pleasure it is to smoke a mild,
good tasting cigarette, they're particular about the brand they choose.
In a repeated, national survey, doctors in all branches of medicine
were asked, "What cigarette do you smoke, doctor?" Time and
again, the brand was Camel. That's right! According to a national
survey, more doctors smoke Camels than any other brand. Why not
change to Camels for the next thirty days and see what a difference
they make in your smoking enjoyment? *(He lights a cigarette and
takes a big drag.)* See how smooth they are on your throat?

> *(The Actor reveals a poster of a doctor
> smoking a cigarette. He flashes a broad smile.
> Lights up on Max working at his desk. Young
> Charlotte, now a teenager, sits in a chair next
> to the radio studying as the commercial
> continues.)*

MAX

How can you study with that trash on?

YOUNG CHARLOTTE

It's the Hit Parade.

> *(Max listens to the commercial for a moment
> with a combination of fascination and dismay.
> The Actor lights a cigarette and takes a long
> drag.)*

ACTOR

Discover how good tasting a cigarette can be. Camels. The cigarette
recommended by doctors.

38

(Max crosses over and switches off the radio in disgust. Lights out on the Actor.)

YOUNG CHARLOTTE

Vati, could you help me with my mathematics?

MAX

I'm working.

YOUNG CHARLOTTE

Please, *Vati*? I've got a test next week and I don't understand how to do the--

MAX

Give it here.

(Max looks at the equations for a moment. He fills in the answers and hands the book back to the disappointed Young Charlotte.)

YOUNG CHARLOTTE

Thank you, *Vati.*

MAX

How is your leg?

YOUNG CHARLOTTE

It's fine.

MAX

You're able to run? No difficulty in gym class?

YOUNG CHARLOTTE

Not anymore.

MAX

You're not smoking at school, are you?

YOUNG CHARLOTTE

No, *Vati.*

MAX

You're sure?

YOUNG CHARLOTTE

Positive.

MAX

Good. See to it that you never do.

SCENE SEVEN.

> *(The bedroom of an upscale, New York
> apartment. Max has just finished examining
> MRS. HAMMERSMITH, a wealthy New York
> matron who is coughing heavily. She lies in
> bed, covered in tumors.)*

MAX

Mrs. Hammersmith, your immune system is already so compromised
from the radiation, the mechlorethamine is making you sicker.

MRS. HAMMERSMITH

Please, doctor. I don't want to die like this. Can't you help me?

MAX

Would you be willing to try something completely different?

MRS. HAMMERSMITH

Anything.

MAX

I want you to stop taking all the drugs Dr. Heller prescribed. And no
more radiation.

40

MRS. HAMMERSMITH
So... I just wait to die?

(Max reaches into his medical bag and hands her a typed list.)

MAX
I want you to try detoxifying your body through nutrition. No foods other than these.

MRS. HAMMERSMITH
No meat? No chocolates?

(Max holds her face in his hand forcefully.)

MAX
If you do exactly as I say, you will get better.

MRS. HAMMERSMITH
I believe you.

(Realizing he's being inappropriate, Max lets go of her face and starts to pack his medical bag.)

MRS. HAMMERSMITH (cont'd)
Dr. Gerson? Thank you for giving me hope.

MAX
Nonsense. I haven't done anything yet.

MRS. HAMMERSMITH
But you have. More than anyone has given me in months.

(She kisses his hand and presses it to her face in deep gratitude. Not knowing how to respond, Max pulls his hand away and starts to exit.)

MAX

I'll see you next week.

(Max exits quickly as she studies the list.)

SCENE EIGHT.

(Crossfade to Max and Rudy's office. Max sits at his desk as Rudy enters with a clipboard.)

RUDY

We're almost out of morphine.

MAX

How could we be out already?

RUDY

Terminal patients need relief.

MAX

They don't need relief. They need hope.

RUDY

You talk that way around the medical board, they'll take away your license.

MAX

I think I've finally perfected this new protocol for cancer patients. The fruit and vegetable juices cleanse the liver, then the organic coffee enemas flush out the toxins.

RUDY

That's a coffee drink I could live without. What drugs go with it?

MAX

None. I put Mrs. Hammersmith on it and her tumors went away.

42

RUDY

Mrs. Hammersmith was my patient. We had an agreement.

MAX

She needed someone right away. You won't do house calls, so I went. The mechlorethamine was making her sicker.

RUDY

And what makes you think she was cured by your Chock Full O' Nuts douches?

MAX

In the ten years we've been in New York, how many of your patients have died?

RUDY

They were terminal when they came to me.

MAX

How many, Rudy?

RUDY

I haven't counted recently.

MAX

Any doctor worth his salt knows exactly.

RUDY
(annoyed)

Twenty-four!

MAX

I've lost one. And that was only because he went off my regimen.

RUDY

You could walk down Park Avenue right now and find a hundred doctors who'll tell you there is no way to cure cancer without drugs.

MAX

That doesn't mean they're right.

RUDY

This might be the reason our practice isn't doing better.

MAX

Yes. It might.

(Max exits. Rudy writes on a form.)

RUDY

I'm ordering a double batch. If our suppliers get wise, we'll be the laughing stock of the medical community.

SCENE NINE.

> *(As Max crosses the stage, city traffic sounds are heard. He sees several current BILLBOARDS: an infant drinking cola out of baby bottle, the benefits of asbestos and the energy boost created by sugar. He pauses for a moment at each one and registers concern. He steps downstage into a harsh spotlight. The authoritative voice of the CHAIRMAN OF THE MEDICAL BOARD is heard in the darkness.)*

CHAIRMAN (V.O.)

Dr. Gerson, this is your second appearance in front of the medical board in the past six months. Is there some problem?

MAX

No, sir. No problem.

CHAIRMAN (V.O.)

Last time, you were proposing alternative types of healing away from our prescribed methodologies.

MAX

That is correct.

CHAIRMAN (V.O.)

And this time, you have stated publicly that smoking contributes to lung disease.

MAX

I have.

CHAIRMAN (V.O.)

But, there is no conclusive proof of this.

(Max takes out a file.)

MAX

Sir, I have ten case histories here that categorically prove that smoking--

CHAIRMAN (V.O.)

Ten cases is hardly substantive evidence.

MAX

If you will give me time, I will produce many more.

CHAIRMAN (V.O.)

Dr. Gerson, does this mean that you refuse to retract your statements?

MAX

It does.

CHAIRMAN (V.O.)

And you are aware you could lose your license?

MAX

On what grounds?

CHAIRMAN (V.O.)

Making false claims.

MAX
(angrily)
They're not false! Maybe your support from the tobacco industry is
the real problem!

CHAIRMAN (V.O.)

What are you implying, sir?

MAX

I'm not implying anything. I know for a fact the president of the
AMA is being paid by the tobacco companies to say that cigarettes
are not harmful! And you're doing the same thing to suppress any
sort of healing that doesn't involve prescription drugs!

*(Sounds of the other doctors screaming in
protest.)*

CHAIRMAN (V.O.)

Dr. Gerson! If you want to retain your medical license, I suggest you
hold your tongue! We will review your case in four months.
Meanwhile, be aware that you will continue to be under close
scrutiny by this organization. Good day, Dr. Gerson.

(A gavel sounds.)

SCENE TEN.

*(Crossfade to Rudy closing up the office for
night. There is a knock on the door. Rudy
opens it and MR. CARMICHAEL, a well-*

46

dressed, thirtysomething businessman, barges in.)

CARMICHAEL

Dr. Gerson?

RUDY

No, I'm Dr. Heller. I'm afraid the office is closed.

CARMICHAEL

I'm sorry to disturb you, doctor. I know an important man like you must want to get home to his family.

RUDY

Do I know you?

(He hands Rudy his card.)

CARMICHAEL

Ralph Carmichael. Riser Pharmaceutical Company.

RUDY

Sir, we are not interested in sampling any new products at the moment. Now, if you'll excuse me--

CARMICHAEL

I understand. But, can I just ask you one question? How many patients do you see in a week?

RUDY

Around 150. Now, I really--

CARMICHAEL

And how many of those are cancer patients?

RUDY

At least half.

CARMICHAEL

What if I were to show you a way you could make an extra five
hundred dollars a month from those patients and see twice as many?

(Rudy studies his face.)

RUDY

You have my attention.

CARMICHAEL

I'm sure you've read in the Journal of The American Medical
Association that the Riser Company has come out with some very
promising new cancer drugs. If you prescribe these to your patients,
we would split the profits 50/50.

RUDY

Have there been clinical trials?

CARMICHAEL

You'd be doing that for us.

RUDY

It sounds dangerous.

CARMICHAEL

Doctor Heller, clearly you're a very moral man. I can understand
why you wouldn't want to put your patients at risk. Not even for an
extra thousand dollars a month.

RUDY

I thought you said 500.

CARMICHAEL

For starters. If things go well, you could double that in no time.

RUDY

I won't take those kinds of chances with my patients.

48

(Rudy starts to go. Carmichael stops him.)

CARMICHAEL

Let me put it another way. What do you like most about being a doctor?

(Rudy ponders this.)

RUDY

The look on someone's face when I take away their pain. It makes me feel...

CARMICHAEL

Like God?

RUDY

Somewhat. Yes.

CARMICHAEL

And then they pay you for it. Pretty well, too?

RUDY

I do alright.

CARMICHAEL

So, an extra thousand a month wouldn't really interest you?

RUDY

I didn't say that.

CARMICHAEL

With all the difficulties your partner's been having lately, this would give you a chance to prove to the AMA that you're a team player.

RUDY

That's Dr. Gerson's matter. No charges were brought against me.

CARMICHAEL

I'm sure you've heard of guilt by association. Kinda like what's going on in Germany right now. The rest of the world thinks every Kraut is either a Nazi or a Jew.

RUDY

There is no correlation whatsoever between--

CARMICHAEL

Don't get me wrong. I love the Germans. Unlike most companies, we still employ some of 'em. Our founder, Gustav Riser, was the personal physician to Emperor Wilhelm the Fourth. Dr. Riser was from Stoodagard.

RUDY

I think you mean Stuttgart.

CARMICHAEL

That's it. You say that with such authority. Stuttgart *(laughs)*. Your language sure can sound harsh, Dr. Hellerbach. Sorry. Heller. You know that look you get when you take away someone's pain? If we work together, you could multiply that look by hundreds. Maybe thousands.

SCENE ELEVEN.

> *(Crossfade to a café table and chairs as Max enters holding a letter.)*

RUDY

Where have you been?

MAX

I had a house call.

RUDY

I thought you were going to stop doing those.

50

MAX

I got a letter from Dr. Schweitzer! I asked him to write me a letter of support for the medical board.

(Max takes the letter out of his pocket and reads.)

MAX (cont'd)

"Dr. Max Gerson cured my wife of untreatable tuberculosis without drugs of any kind. After six months on his regimen, the holes in her lungs completely disappeared. Max Gerson is one of the most eminent geniuses in the history of medicine!"

RUDY
(deadpan)

That's wonderful.

MAX

You don't seem very pleased.

RUDY

Frankly, I'm shocked a man like Albert Schweitzer would discredit himself like that.

MAX

You were there when it happened!

RUDY

And what if I said another doctor collapsed her lung and slowly re-inflated it?

MAX

I'd say you were lying.

RUDY

There's no other way to treat pulmonary tuberculosis.

MAX

Why is it so difficult for you to accept the fact that I cured her? With a letter like this, I'm sure to get the charges dropped and my articles published.

RUDY

What articles?

MAX

That's what prompted the hearing. I've written a few articles on the body's natural ability to heal itself. They wouldn't publish them. But now --

RUDY

Max, listen. It's one thing to do these treatments quietly in your office. It's quite another to have them in print.

MAX

But, Rudy--

RUDY

This is professional suicide. My God, you've already had two hearings!

MAX

Actually, there may be a third. I tried to publish a paper about the harmfulness of smoking, and--

RUDY

Jesus, Max! Don't you know who sponsors the Journal of the AMA? Their principal advertiser is Phillip Morris!

MAX

Of course I know that. That's why I called them on it. They're trying to make the public believe smoking isn't harmful. They're all out to get us, Rudy!

RUDY

Max, are you crazy? Taking on the AMA?

MAX

You know I'm right!

RUDY

You'll be a wonderful a father to Charlotte from inside a jail cell.

MAX

Could they really do that to me?

RUDY

Anything is possible.

MAX
(quietly)
So, you're telling me the AMA is no better than the Nazis?

RUDY

Your words, not mine.

MAX

Who's that salesman who's always hanging around the office?

RUDY

His name's Carmichael. I'm working with him.

(Max stares at Rudy in disgust.)

MAX

Getting kickbacks from a drug salesman for trying experimental drugs? I never thought you'd stoop so low.

RUDY

And how is that any different from your experimentation with carrot juice and coffee enemas?

MAX

Mine is all natural. Yours is poison!

RUDY

You don't know that.

MAX

I won't do it, Rudy! I won't prescribe toxic drugs and say smoking isn't harmful. And I can't work with someone who does.

RUDY

So, you're kicking me out?

(Pause. Both men study each other.)

RUDY (cont'd)

I'll find a new office by the end of the month. Congratulations on your letter from Schweitzer. If you weren't my friend, I'd be jealous.

MAX

Thank you.

RUDY

Maybe I'll look for an office uptown.

MAX

Can you afford that?

RUDY

We'll see.

SCENE TWELVE.

(Two years later. Crossfade to Rudy's elegant office on Park Avenue. Clearly, he has taken a big step up and is doing well. He is just finishing up with Mrs. Hammersmith, the patient in the earlier scene.)

RUDY

Mrs. Hammersmith, I want to increase the dosage of busulfan to four times a day.

MRS. HAMMERSMITH

But doctor, it makes me feel worse. I can't keep any food down.

RUDY

Would you prefer to go back to Dr. Gerson? Wasting away on a diet of twig juice and grass with no pharmaceuticals to help you? I thought you liked your turkey dinners and your mother's chocolate eclairs.

MRS. HAMMERSMITH

I just couldn't stay on that terrible diet any longer.

RUDY

Of course not. I'll give you something to settle your stomach. And let's see if we can keep those lesions from spreading.

(Rudy hands her a prescription.)

MRS. HAMMERSMITH

Do you think I'll live to see Christmas?

RUDY
(smiling)

And Easter. If you do as I say.

MRS. HAMMERSMITH

Thank you, Dr. Heller. You're my savior!

(She embraces Rudy. He accepts the gesture gallantly. As she exits, the speaker on his desk buzzes. Rudy crosses to it.)

RUDY

Yes, Miss Schaeffer?

NURSE (V.O.)

Doctor, there's a woman here without an appointment.

RUDY

My schedule is already backed up.

NURSE (V.O.)

She says it's urgent. Her name is Helga.

RUDY

Send her in.

> (HELGA enters. She is an attractive, well-spoken, curvy, blonde woman in her late twenties. She carries a suitcase.)

RUDY (cont'd)
(in hushed tones)

I told you never to come here.

HELGA

I had nowhere else to go. My landlady threw me out.

RUDY

Why?

HELGA

She caught me turning tricks again.

RUDY

Don't be vulgar.

HELGA

Have it your way. She caught me entertaining a gentleman friend.
Said I had to get out or she was going to triple the rent.

RUDY

She can't do that!

HELGA
(smirks)
Do you want to call the housing board or shall I?

RUDY

No relatives?

HELGA

A great aunt in Krakow. She's 93.

RUDY

No one else?

HELGA

Do you think I'd be here if there were? I'll have to leave town
otherwise.

RUDY

You can't leave! Where would I find another--?

HELGA

Then, why not play house for awhile?

(Rudy thinks it over.)

HELGA (cont'd)
If you let me stay, you can do whatever you want. No charge.

*(Rudy reaches into his desk and hands her a
key.)*

RUDY

You can stay for one week. If you see the superintendent, you're my
cousin from Gdansk. I'll see what I can do to find you another place.

HELGA

Thank you, my darling. You're a life saver. I'll cook and clean and
take good care of you.

(Helga unzips his trousers.)

RUDY

Not here!

HELGA

We can make it fast.

(Helga gets on her knees in front of Rudy. Just as she is undoing his belt, Carmichael enters.)

CARMICHAEL
(smiling)
Now, that ought to be better than a dose of penicillin!

(Helga quickly rises as Rudy fixes his belt.)

RUDY
(flustered)
Mr. Carmichael! Did we have an appointment?

CARMICHAEL

Obviously not.

RUDY

Mr. Carmichael, this is Helga.

HELGA
(grandly)
How do you do? I'm his cousin from Gdansk.

CARMICHAEL
(laughing)
Your cousin, huh?

RUDY

She was just leaving.

(Helga quickly exits.)

RUDY (cont'd)

Now, what can I do for you?

CARMICHAEL

Nothing as interesting as that, I can promise you. I'm here about your former colleague.

RUDY

What about him?

CARMICHAEL

Are you aware of the article Dr. Gerson published in the New York Journal of Medicine? He claims to be curing cancer without drugs.

RUDY

I knew he was thinking of publishing, but I didn't--

CARMICHAEL

You knew about this?

RUDY

I haven't seen him in nearly two years.

CARMICHAEL

If people start believing information like this, it could be very dangerous.

RUDY

Mr. Carmichael, most lay people don't read medical journals.

CARMICHAEL

Doctors do. And they're the ones who buy drugs.

RUDY

True, but--

CARMICHAEL

I wonder if he has any proof of this.

RUDY

He must. Max always kept meticulous records.

CARMICHAEL

Yeah? Sure wish I could see some of them. It would really help our case. Yours too.

RUDY

Mine?

CARMICHAEL

As his former partner. It'd be terrible if you were implicated in any of the charges against him.

RUDY

I never had anything to do with--

CARMICHAEL

I believe you. And I'm sure the records would prove that.

RUDY

How many cases would you need to see?
CARMICHAEL
I dunno. Say...fifteen?

RUDY

He'd never give me that many!

CARMICHAEL

Ten, then. By next Thursday.

RUDY

I'll see what I can do.

CARMICHAEL

You know, if you increase the dosage on those experimental drugs, we could start increasing your profits.

                              RUDY
No, thank you.

                           CARMICHAEL
You'd be performing a great service for humanity.

                              RUDY
                            (angrily)
Humanity?! You're not here when my patients come to me
dehydrated, riddled with tumors and dying faster than they have any
right to. I have to look them in the eye and prescribe something that I
know won't work just so you can complete one of your damned
studies!

                           CARMICHAEL
Doc, I'm not asking you to do anything unethical. It must be terrible
watching people die everyday.

                              RUDY
I'm not doing this anymore.

                           CARMICHAEL
I can understand how you feel. I bet the strain it causes is something
awful. And living here in New York must add to the anxiety.

                              RUDY
What does that have to do--?

                           CARMICHAEL
Ever hear of a doctor named Johan Hilligoss? He couldn't take the
stress of the city anymore. The noise, the subways, the crowds. He
set up a practice down in Mobile. After about a month, these guys in
white sheets sliced his throat with is own scalpel. Burned his house
to the ground. His wife suffered third degree burns and his cocker
spaniel died of asphyxiation. Just because they didn't like his last
name.

RUDY
(after a pause.)
I'll have the files for you next week.

(Carmichael extends his hand and smiles.)

CARMICHAEL
Always a pleasure doing business, Dr. Hellerbach.

RUDY

It's Heller.

CARMICHAEL
(smiling)

Sure it is.

(Carmichael exits. Visibly shaken, Rudy stares out the window.)

SCENE THIRTEEN.

(Lights crossfade to the café. Rudy and Max sit facing each other sipping coffee.)

MAX
Mmmm! This coffee is incredible! I haven't tasted anything like it since we left Hamburg.

RUDY
It's from that little place we used to go on the Linder Strasse. I ordered it months ago.

MAX
(joyfully)
The Linder Strasse! How on earth could you get coffee all the way from Hamburg?

RUDY

I have my ways.

MAX

What was the name of that waitress? The one who was in love with me. Always wore the low cut blouse?

RUDY

With the face like a mud fence? Otka!

MAX
(laughing)
Otka! How could I forget? Remember that time she was serving you a plate of poached eggs and she leaned over so far, her left tit fell out!

RUDY

And I said, "Thank you Otka, but I can only eat two poached eggs at a time!" She was so embarrassed, she went back to the kitchen and wouldn't come out until we left!

(The two men laugh raucously.)

MAX

I've missed you, my friend.

RUDY (cont'd)

And I've missed you.

MAX

Why did you stay away so long?

RUDY

It won't happen again. How's Charlotte?

MAX

Wonderful. In a boarding school upstate.

RUDY

I'm surprised you'd let her go away.

MAX

It was all getting to be too much for her.

RUDY

I don't understand.

MAX

There was a child of one of the doctors I'd spoken out against at her school. When she came home with a black eye...

(Rudy looks shocked.)

MAX (cont'd)

You know how cruel children can be.

RUDY

Almost as bad as their parents?

MAX

The tuition stretches me to the limit, but I can't have them attacking her, too.

RUDY

They go after the thing you love the most and still you persist?

MAX

Do you think it was easy? Charlotte is all I have in the world.

RUDY

Then why not--?

MAX

My friend. Please.

(Rudy stirs his coffee.)

                              RUDY

How's business, Max?

                              MAX

Slow.

                              RUDY

Your articles didn't help?

                              MAX

You read my articles?

                              RUDY

Of course.

                              MAX

And...?

                              RUDY

I think you're very brave. Especially since it's made you a laughing
stock among your colleagues.

                              MAX

Do you really believe that?

                              RUDY

I don't want to. But when I go to medical conferences and seminars,
people talk. Some think your license should be revoked.

                              MAX

Do you?

                              RUDY

Max, if you'd be willing to share some of your case histories with
me, I could talk to people. Set the record straight.

                              MAX

But, you've never believed in my methods.

RUDY

While we've been apart, I've had some time to think. Perhaps I need to learn more about them.

MAX

Rudy, I can't tell you how happy this makes me!

RUDY

So, you'll get me the files? Some of your best cases?

MAX

I can't let them out of the office. But you're welcome to come by and read them whenever you like.

RUDY

You couldn't let me take them? Just for a few days?

MAX

What if something were to--?

RUDY

It's a shame you don't trust the man who saved your life.

(Max hesitates.)

RUDY (cont'd)

And Charlotte's.

MAX

Call my receptionist in the morning.

SCENE FOURTEEN.

(Crossfade to Rudy's apartment. Helga is listening to a Benny Goodman tune and

66

*jitterbugging by herself. Rudy enters the scene
and makes notes on Max's files.)*

RUDY

Do you have to do that now?

HELGA

You said we were going dancing tonight.

RUDY

I've got to make notes on these files.

*(Rudy crosses to the record player and
switches it off.)*

HELGA

But we haven't been out in so long!

RUDY

We went to the botanical gardens on Sunday.

HELGA

That's not going out! You told me the Latin names of all the
butterflies until I thought I'd turn blue.

RUDY

Nobody's holding a gun to your head to stay here.

HELGA

So, you'd rather I left?

RUDY

Don't be stupid.

(Rudy stays buried in his files.)

HELGA

What's the matter, lover? Don't I please you anymore?

RUDY

Of course.

HELGA

Do you think I'm pretty?

RUDY

Very.

*(Helga wraps her arms around Rudy and
starts kissing him on the neck. He pulls her
off.)*

RUDY (cont'd)

I have to finish these.

HELGA

Did you like the schnitzel I made tonight?

RUDY

Very tasty.

HELGA

There's some left over. I thought I'd take it down the hall to Mrs.
Lewis. She's got a terrible cold and--

RUDY

I don't want you talking to the neighbors.

HELGA

What harm could--?

RUDY

People gossip. I have a reputation to maintain.

HELGA

But, I get so bored and lonely here all day.

RUDY

The movie theatre is two blocks away.

HELGA

I've seen that movie. Twice. Putting Santa Claus on trial for insanity. It's ridiculous! And that little girl whines all the time!

RUDY

I mean it, Helga! I don't want you talking to people in the building.

HELGA

I heard you!

(Bored, she picks up one of Rudy's files.)

HELGA (cont'd)

Natural healing? That's what kept my grandpa Oskar alive for another seven years.

RUDY

You don't know what you're talking about.

(Rudy snatches the file out of her hands. She grabs it back.)

HELGA

Actually, I know quite a bit about it. I used to help my grandmother prepare his special meals. After a few weeks, he stopped coughing and his color came back. His doctors said it was a miracle.

RUDY

(Laughs)

And there were probably fairies in his garden, too!

(Rudy puts the music back on.)

HELGA

It saved him.

RUDY

Have you ever seen a Broadway show? I could take you next week.

HELGA

A musical?

RUDY

Perhaps.

HELGA

Can we go see *Finian's Rainbow*? I heard one of the songs on the radio.

RUDY

It's sold out for the next six months.

(*Helga crosses to Rudy and embraces him seductively.*)

HELGA

But you can do it. The great and powerful Doctor Heller can do anything.

RUDY
(*with a lecherous grin*)

Anything?

(*Rudy starts nibbling Helga's neck. She laughs.*)

SCENE FIFTEEN.

(*Crossfade to Max sitting in a recording studio with LONG JOHN NEBEL, a nice looking, middle-aged man with a fluid speaking voice.*)

70

LONG JOHN

Welcome back. You're listening to the Long John Nebel Late Night Show and I'm concluding my exclusive interview with Dr. Max Gerson, author of the upcoming book, *A Cancer Therapy*. The phones have been going crazy here at the studio, but I'm going to defer any more callers so I can get to the bottom of something. Dr. Gerson, if you really have a solution for cancer - and I'm not saying you do - but if you do, why isn't the AMA publishing your work?

MAX

Why do <u>you</u> think, Mr. Nebel?

LONG JOHN

Well, if they think that you're...and I don't want to use too strong a word here...a fake, wouldn't they just throw you out?

MAX

I have been investigated five times by the Medical Society of the County of New York. But I bring them patients the investigators themselves sent home to die.

LONG JOHN

What were the results of the investigation?

MAX

They won't release them. To me or to anyone else.

LONG JOHN

And what do you think is the reason?

MAX

Their unwillingness to admit that I cured these people. And not only cancer. I believe it is possible to cure any disease known to man without drugs.

LONG JOHN

That's quite a claim, Dr. Gerson. What do you consider to be the cause of most degenerative diseases?

MAX

Big American corporations.

LONG JOHN
(confused)

I'm sorry, I don't under--

MAX

The companies that make processed and refined foods. They take everything natural out of the food and make it synthetic. The same is true with the makers of artificial fertilizers and chemicals. With no nutrients in the soil, how can we grow anything worthwhile? And of course, the makers of tobacco and alcohol.

LONG JOHN

I want to make it perfectly clear that the opinions being expressed are those of Dr. Gerson and not belonging to myself or WOR radio. Do they acknowledge you in Europe, Dr. Gerson?

MAX

Some doctors do. Most do not. At least my method is accepted there as a valid alternative.

LONG JOHN

We're out of time, but this has been absolutely fascinating. I have many more questions and I'm sure our listeners do, too. Can you come back next week?

MAX

It would be my great pleasure.

LONG JOHN

Ladies and gentlemen, Max Gerson wants to give information to others in his profession, but they are reluctant to accept it. I'm not a medical expert. People listening can make their own decision. But I will say this. You should remember this name: Doctor Max Gerson.

LONG JOHN (cont'd)

We will eagerly await his upcoming book, A Cancer Therapy. This is Long John Nebel saying thank you and good night.

(Long John rises and shakes Max's hand.)

Doc, that was amazing!

MAX

Thank you, Mr. Nebel.

(A SECRETARY enters and hands Long John a large stack of messages.)

LONG JOHN

Will you look at all these calls! I've never seen anything like this. *(Thumbing through them)* appointment requests, book orders...you're going to be one popular man, Dr. Gerson.

MAX
(reaching for them)

Thank you. May I...?

LONG JOHN

Sorry, I can't give them to you just yet. Company policy. My boss needs to see them first. He uses these to track the ratings. I'll give them all to you next week.

MAX

I understand.

LONG JOHN

And to think I just interviewed the man who cured cancer!

(Long John shakes Max's hand again. Max smiles.)

SCENE SIXTEEN.

(Lights crossfade to Rudy's office. Carmichael stands there.)

CARMICHAEL

Why didn't you tell me he was writing a book?

RUDY

I didn't think it was important.

CARMICHAEL

Not important?

RUDY

How much harm could it do?

CARMICHAEL

Doc, just think about this for a second. You and all your colleagues are out there busting your asses curing people in the traditional way. Then Max Gerson comes along and says, "The methods you've been using for years are no good. Don't take those drugs, just eat a few stalks of celery instead." Frankly, I didn't think you were the type of guy who liked being laughed at.

RUDY

Laughed at...?

CARMICHAEL

You don't see how he's mocking you?

RUDY

Max Gerson would not--

CARMICHAEL

Actions speak louder than words.

RUDY

But, why would he--?

CARMICHAEL

You still don't get how dangerous this man is, do you? What if next
week, say half - no, a third. A third of the cancer patients in
Manhattan went to their oncologists and said, "Thanks all the same,
doc. I'm gonna try to cure my cancer naturally." One third fewer
drugs are getting sold. The drug manufacturers take a hit. Then one
third of the pharmacies go out of business. Those pharmacists can't
feed their kids, which affects the grocers, the landlords, the retail
stores. The entire infrastructure starts to collapse. And that's not even
taking into account the impact it would have on your own practice.
A smaller office, no receptionist, no trips in the summer. All of a
sudden you're walking down Park Avenue and someone whispers,
"That's Rudolph Heller. He used to be a great doctor. Then he was
destroyed by some nut who claimed he could cure cancer without
drugs. And all that happens because Max Gerson publishes a book
you didn't think was important.

(Pause. Rudy considers this a moment.)

RUDY

I'll stop the book.

CARMICHAEL

How?

RUDY

I'll find a way.

CARMICHAEL

You're a good guy, Doc.

(Rudy forces a smile as Carmichael exits.)

SCENE SEVENTEEN.

*(Max crosses to Rudy at the café and angrily
tosses a medical journal on the table.)*

MAX

Did you see the editorial in the last edition of the Journal? It states
quite clearly that there is no indication whatsoever that nutrition
affects cancer. I'm thinking of suing.

RUDY

On what grounds?

MAX

Slander. Defamation of character.

RUDY

Do they mention you by name?

MAX

They don't need to! Everyone knows this is in response to my work.
They heard the broadcast.

RUDY

Max, I can understand why you'd be upset but --

MAX

Upset?! Their greed is destroying my life's work! All because there's
no money in it!

RUDY

Max, if the AMA says there is no connection --

MAX

Then they're idiots! And anyone who believes it is too!

RUDY
(quietly)

So, you're saying I'm an idiot?

MAX

No, I--

RUDY

You are, aren't you?

MAX

My friend. Just listen to me. That fancy, red Packard you've been wanting to buy. What would you put in the tank?

RUDY
(patiently)

High octane gasoline.

MAX

Suppose you put Coca-Cola in it instead? Would you expect it to run?

RUDY

Don't be ridiculous.

MAX

Then how can we expect our bodies to run on sugary drinks, processed foods and fatty meats? The cultures with most longevity have always lived on fruits, vegetables and grains.

RUDY

Max, I see your point, but--

MAX
(raising his voice)

No, you don't, Rudy!

RUDY

Shhhh!

MAX
(more quietly)
They're calling me a quack simply because I'm not prescribing
expensive, toxic drugs and costly surgery. I'm publishing my book
even if it takes my last breath. These people are crooks and I am not
going to stop until I prove them wrong!

RUDY
So, now I'm an idiot <u>and</u> a crook?

MAX
I didn't mean--

RUDY
I saved your life and this is how you repay me? By mocking me, by
trying to take down the very institution of medicine?

MAX
Can't you see how they're trying to destroy us?

RUDY
No. But I see how <u>you</u> are!

*(Rudy rises from the table and speaks
with quiet intensity.)*

RUDY (cont'd)
You're a dangerous man, Max Gerson. Deluded, unstable and
dangerous!

*(Rudy walks quickly away from the table. Max
watches him go in shock.)*

(Lights crossfade to Rudy and Helga at the theatre. An actor and an actress in Victorian era costumes are doing the final scene from Act III of "Hedda Gabler", playing EILERT LOVBORG and HEDDA GABLER. There is a stage fireplace on the set. We cannot hear the dialogue at first, as the scene is from Helga's point of view.)

HELGA

This is such a talky play!

RUDY

Shh! It's a classic! You must try to concentrate.

HELGA

Then, you shouldn't have given me so much wine at dinner.

(Helga belches, then giggles.)

RUDY

Behave yourself.

(We now hear the scene onstage.)

EILERT LOVBORG

"Suppose that a man, in the small hours of the morning, came home to his child's mother after a night of riot and debauchery and said: 'Listen, I have been here and there, and I have taken our child with me. And I have lost the child - utterly lost it. The devil knows into what hands it may have fallen - who may have had their clutches on it.'"

HEDDA GABLER

"But when all is said and done, it was only a book."

EILERT LOVBORG

"My entire soul was in that book."

HEDDA GABLER

"So, you've lost it. What path do you mean to take then?"

EILERT LOVBORG

"None. I will only try to make an end of it all—the sooner the better."

HEDDA GABLER

"Yes. I understand."

(Helga squirms in her seat. The actors go mute.)

HELGA

Why is this Hedda Gabler such a bitch, anyway?

RUDY

Language! You're not in the brothel anymore.

HELGA

At least there I got to sleep sometimes. You snore like a freight train. That is, when you're not poking me with your big—

RUDY

Be quiet!

(Helga sticks her tongue out at Rudy then turns back to face the actors. Hedda Gabler hands Eilert Lovborg a pistol.)

EILERT LOVBORG

"Is this the memento?"

HEDDA GABLER

"Do you recognize it? It was aimed at you once."

EILERT LOVBORG

"You should have used it then."

HEDDA GABLER

"Take it. And use it now."

HELGA
(alarmed)

Does she want him to --?

RUDY

Shh!

HEDDA GABLER

"And do it beautifully, Eilert Lovborg! Promise me that!"

(Eilert Lovborg nods and starts to head offstage. Helga and Rudy are both transfixed.)

HEDDA GABLER

"Vine leaves! You'll have vine leaves in your hair!"

(Eilert Lovborg exits. Hedda Gabler crosses to the fireplace. A gunshot is heard offstage. She reveals a hidden manuscript and rips the pages out, tossing them into the fire. Helga is moved to tears.)

HEDDA GABLER

"I'm killing your child, Eilert Lovborg! I'm killing your child!"

(Rudy is totally focused on the actress.)

HEDDA GABLER (cont'd)

"I'm killing your child!"

(As the actress shoves more pages into the fire, Rudy watches her intently, rising from his seat. Helga turns to Rudy with concern as the lights start to dim.)

END OF ACT ONE

Noah Wagner as Rudolph Heller and David Sasik as Carmichael in the original production of
The Man Who Killed the Cure.

David Sasik, Melissa Musial, Tom Juarez, Jordan Kay and Ashley Rose in the original
production of
The Man Who Killed the Cure.

(Photo credit: Paul Kennedy)

ACT TWO

PROLOGUE.

(Rudy addresses the audience.)

RUDY

The dictionary defines the word "trust" as "assured reliance on the character, ability, strength, or truth of someone or something." Such a powerful feeling. It's astonishing, really, what you can accomplish when someone trusts you completely. On rare occasions, I'd ask myself, "My God. What if Max Gerson is right? What if he really can heal people without drugs? Suppose he could be the one to change the face of modern medicine?" Usually, a good bowel movement would make the feeling pass.

SCENE ONE.

(A few days later. The café. Max and Rudy sit at their regular table. Max sips coffee.)

MAX

And he had a stack of messages as big as my thumb! All with people wanting book requests and appointments!

RUDY

Max, to insult the AMA on the radio when you're already under investigation...

MAX

When am I not under investigation? Besides, what better arena to plead my case?

(Rudy starts to pour Max another cup of coffee.)

MAX (cont'd)

Thank you, no more.

RUDY

Why?

MAX

My stomach is a bit off today.

RUDY

This is just what you need to settle it. Add some milk.

(Max takes the coffee.)

MAX

Aren't you having any?

RUDY

I can't drink coffee anymore. It makes me too jittery.

MAX

I haven't heard you talk about the ladies lately. Any new conquests?

RUDY

Not in awhile. And you? Still living like a monk?

MAX

My work is my mistress. Besides, Charlotte will be living with me in a few months on her summer vacation. She's going to help me in the office. Wants to learn about natural healing.

RUDY

How is the book coming along?

MAX

It's so hard to find the time. And my typing is pathetic.

                    RUDY
Why not hire a typist?

                    MAX
That's an extravagance I can't afford.

                    RUDY
Suppose I paid for it?

                    MAX
Rudy, I couldn't let you do that.

                    RUDY
Why not?

                    MAX
I'm not a charity case.

                    RUDY
Max, will you put your stupid pride aside for once? I want to do this
for you. As a gift. It would give me great pleasure.

                    MAX
That's very generous of you.

                    RUDY
Anything to help you finish your book.

                    MAX
Thank you, my friend.

                    RUDY
I know the perfect girl. Young. Smart. Not bad to look at, either. I'll
have her call you to work out the details.

                    MAX
Wonderful.

RUDY

Same time Thursday?

MAX

Yes.

(The two men shake hands. Rudy exits. As Max crosses the stage, he sees the doctor/Camel ad. This time, the doctor has sunken cheeks and a deathly look. Max turns away and rubs his eyes.
As he looks back at the billboard, it looks normal.)

SCENE TWO.

(Crossfade to Rudy's apartment. That night. Helga enters drying her hands on a dishtowel, followed by Rudy.)

HELGA

Let me think about it.

RUDY

I've already told him you'd do it.

HELGA

Without even asking me? So, now you're pimping me out?

RUDY

This is strictly business. When you meet with him, tell him your typewriter is too heavy to carry back and forth. You'll type the pages at home and give them back to him the next day.

HELGA

And then?

RUDY

Bring them here to me.

HELGA

What will you do with them?

RUDY

Just do as I ask.

HELGA

Not unless you tell me.

RUDY

I'm helping him rewrite the book.

HELGA

Then why don't you tell him that?

RUDY

He's too proud. His English grammar is terrible and he won't ask for help.

HELGA

What are you not telling me?

RUDY

Don't you trust me?

HELGA

I want to.

RUDY

Then it's settled.

(Rudy caresses her cheek.)

HELGA

I don't feel like it tonight, Rudy.

RUDY

Since when?

(Rudy kisses her. Helga reluctantly responds.)

RUDY (cont'd)

That's my pretty, little whore.

HELGA
(pulling away)

Don't call me that!

RUDY

I was teasing, *liebchen*. You're too delicate. (Pause) Come sit on my lap.

(Helga reluctantly does so.)

RUDY (cont'd)

When was the last time I told you that you're beautiful?

HELGA

Never, actually.

(Rudy starts kissing her.)

RUDY

Well, you are. You're like a lovely Christmas stollen stuffed with apricots and dates.

HELGA
(laughs)

You're not much of a poet.

(Helga put her arms around his neck and kisses him.)

SCENE THREE.

(Crossfade to Max walking down the street, later that night. Long John enters.)

MAX

Mr. Nebel! I thought I was supposed to meet you at the studio.

LONG JOHN

You were. I was trying to meet you before you got there.

MAX

I'm not late, am I?

LONG JOHN

No. The president of the station called me into his office today. All of our sponsors have pulled out.

MAX

Your sponsors...?

LONG JOHN

Hostess cupcakes. Phillip Morris. Oscar Meyer. Miller High Life. All the companies you said cause cancer.

MAX

I didn't say--

LONG JOHN

You may as well have. Those accounts represent tens of thousands to WOR. The president told me hell would freeze over before he'd ever let you back on the air.

MAX

I'm terribly sorry to have caused you any trouble, Mr. Nebel. Perhaps if you explain to your listeners--

LONG JOHN

Doc. I don't have any more listeners. He fired me.

MAX

How could it be your fault?

LONG JOHN

Apparently, my tone and manner implied I was supporting your views. He said no one would ever believe me if I did another plug for Chesterfields or Twinkies.

MAX

But, what about all those calls? The messages from your listeners?

LONG JOHN

He threw them down the incinerator. I'm sorry.

MAX

So am I.

LONG JOHN

After all these years, they had an armed guard escort me out of the building. I haven't had the guts to tell my wife yet.

MAX

You're a decent man, Mr. Nebel.

(Max shakes his hand.)

LONG JOHN

It's a shame the world doesn't celebrate decent men.

SCENE FOUR.

(Crossfade to Max's Office. Max is working at his desk as Helga enters with some typed pages.)

HELGA

Hello? Dr. Gerson?

MAX

Helga!

HELGA

I just wanted to drop off these pages.

MAX

I was just having some tea. May I offer you a cup?

HELGA

Thank you. You're very kind.

> *(Max pours her a cup of tea and looks through
> the new pages.)*

MAX

Please have a seat. How are things at home?

HELGA

Fine, thank you.

MAX

Is your mother's cough any better?

HELGA
(Hesitantly)

About the same.

MAX

Helga, I'm wondering if you're getting enough sleep.

HELGA

Why?

MAX

There seem to be some...irregularities in these pages. Perhaps my
dictation is not as accurate as it might--

HELGA

Your dictation is fine.

MAX

For instance, here on page 143, you typed the patient's symptoms were rampant. I said they were in remission.

HELGA
(Confused)

I did?

MAX

And there seems to be a whole section missing on page 150 where I talk about the speed of her recovery.

HELGA

That's strange. I'll listen to the tape again.

MAX

Would you? I'd certainly appreciate it. Do you think you could double check the ones from today as well?

(Max hands her back the pages.)

HELGA

If you'd like me to.

MAX

I think I'd rest easier. Thank you so much, Helga.

HELGA

If I may say, doctor, I think what you're doing is wonderful. The world needs more men like you.

MAX

Thank you, Helga. That means a great deal.

HELGA

But, how do you think you cured all those people when their doctors said they were going to die?

MAX

The others saw them as numbers. I saw them as people. Helping them to believe that they could heal was more than anything I ever did.

HELGA

But, you saved their lives!

MAX

They saved themselves. I just gave them hope. Good night, Helga.

(Helga stares at Max for a moment as if she'd just seen an angel. She starts to say something, then exits quickly.)

SCENE FIVE.

(Crossfade to Rudy's apartment. Classical music plays on the hi-fi. A portion of Max's manuscript is on the table. Rudy's face is buried in the pages. Helga enters and switches off the music.)

HELGA

I had a cup of tea with Doctor Gerson today.

RUDY

Oh?

HELGA

He was asking me questions about where I lived.

RUDY

You didn't tell him anything?

HELGA

Of course not. But I'm curious about something.

RUDY

Well?

HELGA

Why are you trying to ruin him?

RUDY

What?

HELGA

You told me you were correcting his spelling and grammar.

RUDY

I just want to be sure--

HELGA

Rudy, I know what you're doing. So does he.

RUDY

Then you'll have to be more careful, won't you?

HELGA

You're destroying his book. Why would you do such a thing, Rudy?

RUDY

I told you, that's my business.

HELGA

Until yesterday, you were just reading it. He spotted your changes right away. And he thinks it's my fault.

RUDY

Helga, you'd do well to stay out of this. If you need more money, I'll--

HELGA

It's not about the money. I think you're jealous of him.

RUDY

Why would I--?

HELGA

You know he's a real healer and you're not!

RUDY

What gives you the right to say that to me?!

HELGA

Look me in the eye and tell me it's not true.

RUDY

I got you a job. You should be thanking me.

HELGA

Thanking you? For ruining Max Gerson's life?

RUDY

Don't be so melodramatic.

HELGA

I'm not doing this anymore.

RUDY

You don't know him. He's shooting himself in the foot with this book. This is what's best for him.

HELGA

What if he really does have a cure for cancer?

RUDY

He's a quack. He's doing more harm than good!

HELGA

He a genius! He's twice the man you'll ever be!

RUDY

Really? And which whorehouse taught you such fine breeding?

(Helga spits in his face. Pause.)

RUDY (cont'd)

You're in love with him!

HELGA

Don't be stupid.

RUDY

You shared a cup of tea. Did you share his bed?

HELGA

That would drive you insane, wouldn't it?

RUDY

You little slut!

HELGA

What if I made Max Gerson my new lover?

RUDY

Before I'd let that happen, I'd...

HELGA

What? Kill me? I'd have been better off in Auschwitz than to stay with you!

RUDY

You ungrateful, little bitch!

(He stands in front of her with a wild look in his eyes. Rudy takes a PISTOL out of a drawer and holds it up to Helga.)

HELGA

Go ahead! Do it! Kill me!

(Dropping the pistol, Rudy screams in frustration and throws himself onto the sofa. Helga rises and crosses to the door.)

RUDY

Where are you going?

HELGA

For a walk. The air is putrid in here.

(Helga puts on her coat and hat.)

RUDY

Liebchen, next Saturday night...a musical?

HELGA

We'll see.

(Helga exits. After a beat, Rudy crosses to Max's manuscript on the table. He picks up a page and tears it to shreds.)

RUDY

I'm killing your child, Max Gerson! I'm killing your child!

(Rudy picks up another page, crumples it and eats it like a wild animal. He spits the half-eaten page onto the floor.)

SCENE SIX.

(Lights up on Max and Helga walking along the street.)

HELGA

It's very kind of you to walk me home, Dr. Gerson.

MAX

Nonsense. You're doing so much for me.

HELGA

Not really.

MAX

If you like, I could stop in and take a look at your mother. Perhaps I could prescribe something for her cough.

HELGA

No! Thank you.

MAX

I wouldn't charge you.

HELGA

Actually, she's feeling much better. But I appreciate the offer.

MAX

Is this your street?

HELGA

Yes.

MAX

Is that how you know Rudy? From the neighborhood?

HELGA

Who?

MAX

Dr. Heller. He lives up here as well.

HELGA
(Uneasy)

Does he?

MAX

I must say, I'm a little envious you live in such a nice neighborhood.
I can't afford anything up here. Perhaps once my book is published...

HELGA

Well, good night.

MAX
(Hesitantly)

Helga, before you go, I was wondering...may I take you to dinner
sometime?

HELGA

Dr. Gerson, I--

MAX

Don't you think it's time you called me Max?

HELGA

I'm sorry...

MAX
(smiling)

Of course. You have a boyfriend. A pretty girl like you, I should
have known. I'm sorry, I...I've been so lonely since my wife died.
Sometimes I forget myself.

HELGA

I'd love to.

MAX

What?

HELGA

I'd love to have dinner with you. You're one of the kindest men I've ever met.

> (*Helga kisses Max tenderly, then passionately. He holds her too tightly, pressing up against her. Helga breaks away. They stare at each other for a moment.*)

HELGA (cont'd)

Can we go right now?

MAX
> (*flustered*)

To dinner? Of course. Have you ever been to Luchow's?

SCENE SEVEN.

> (*Crossfade to a downstage table with elegant place settings and crystal. An orchestra plays in the background. Max and Helga stand by the entrance, waiting for a table.*)

HELGA

What a lovely place!

MAX

It's the best German food outside of Hamburg. You must try the pumpernickel.

HELGA

That waiter! His tray is on fire!

MAX
(laughing)
That's a flaming cherries jubilee. The waiter douses the cherries in
Kirschwasser and lights it at your table.

HELGA
I'm so stupid.

MAX
(beaming)
You're charming.

HELGA
No one's ever said that to me before.

> *(Max and Helga cross to a table. Once they
> are seated, Max addresses a WAITER.)*

MAX
Waiter! Cherries Jubilee for two! And a bottle of your best
champagne!

> *(The waiter nods and exits.)*

MAX (cont'd)
This is a special occasion. Why not have dessert first?

HELGA
(joyously)
Why not?
(They both laugh.)

MAX
I'm sorry to bring us both back down to earth, but before I forget, I
thought of another change I want to make on the new pages.

HELGA
Let me go powder my nose and then I'll make a note.

(Helga exits.)

SCENE EIGHT.

> *(Crossfade to the ladies' lounge at Luchow's.
> An ATTENDANT sits there with a tray of
> perfumes. Helga peruses them.)*

HELGA

What's something an older man would like?

ATTENDANT

To forget that he's old. Try this one.

> *(She dabs some perfume on Helga's wrist.
> Helga smells it, smiles and nods.)*

ATTENDANT (cont'd)

Wait a minute.

> *(The attendant sprays Helga with perfume and
> brushes her hair in the back.)*

ATTENDANT (cont'd)

Now you're perfect. Go get him, *schatzie*!

> *(Helga laughs gaily as she hands her a dollar
> bill and exits.)*

SCENE NINE.

> *(Helga returns to the table and sees Max
> studying the manuscript. He is quietly
> seething with anger.)*

HELGA

Doctor Gerson, I can explain...

MAX
(quietly)
Who do you work for, Helga? These notations are not in your
handwriting. Someone must be paying you to destroy my
manuscript. Is it the AMA? A pharmaceutical company? Or a Nazi
sympathizer? I know I have a lot of enemies. Which one would
stoop so low?

HELGA
Dr. Gerson, I swear to you, I didn't know at first--

MAX
But then you did. And you kept on. Why, Helga? Have you enjoyed
playing me for a fool?

HELGA
It's not like that.

MAX
Then what, Helga? There is nothing more important to me than this
work. This book might have saved others. You're nothing short of a
murderer.

HELGA
I'm not! I... *(Pause.)* Do you really want to know who it is?

MAX
I don't suppose it matters. Dr. Heller will be so upset. He sent you
to me as a gift. *(Pause.)* I quite enjoyed our moment on the street
today. I didn't know it was the kiss of Judas.

> *(The waiter enters with the Cherries Jubilee.*
> *Max grabs the manuscript and hurls it into the*
> *cherry syrup. Max turns to the waiter.)*

MAX (cont'd)
Light it.

HELGA

You can't--

MAX

I said light it!

HELGA

No!

(Helga grabs the manuscript and clutches it. Her hands are covered in cherry syrup. Max snaps his fingers at the waiter who exits abruptly. Max rises from the table.)

MAX

I said you were nothing short of a murderer. At least now you look the part. Goodbye, Helga.

(Max hurls a few bills on the table and exits. The stunned Helga tries to wipe the manuscript clean, as if she were handling a wounded animal. She stares down at her hands covered in cherry syrup as the lights slowly fade.)

SCENE TEN.

(Crossfade to Rudy's apartment.)

RUDY

Of course, when she told me, I threw her out. What choice did I have? It was clear she was in love with him. Helga was no use to me anymore and whores are a dime a dozen.

(Rudy reaches for his checkbook as Helga enters carrying a suitcase.)

105

RUDY (cont'd)

I'll just make this out to "cash", shall I? And take your noisy records, too.

HELGA

I have nothing to play them on.

RUDY

They don't have a hi-fi at the whorehouse?

(Rudy hands her the check. Helga takes it reluctantly and exits into the bedroom. Rudy calls to her.)

RUDY (cont'd)

You still have your looks. You'll find someone else. But you'd best cut down on the pastries. They're starting to show on your hips. I'll take your suitcase downstairs.

(Rudy exits with the suitcase. Helga enters in a hat and coat. She takes out a folded note and leaves it on the table. She exits. After a moment, Rudy re-enters and reads the note.)

RUDY (cont'd)

"Tell Dr. Gerson I'm sorry." Not me. Max! Her last words to me were about him! After all I did for her, this is how she repays me! Of course, I knew now that when she said she loved me she was lying. A desperate plea to stop me from kicking her to the curb. Still, she was...

(He puts his hand to his face for a moment, then laughs.)

SCENE ELEVEN.

(Rudy crosses to Max at the café. Max sips his coffee.)

RUDY

Do you have any idea who she was working for?

MAX

There are a lot of people who'd like to see me stopped.

RUDY

Max, I feel so responsible.

MAX

Nonsense. It's not your fault, my friend.

(Max stares at an unseen man at a nearby table.)

MAX (cont'd)

Is he staring at me?

RUDY

Who?

MAX

Him. I'm being followed all the time.

RUDY

I don't think so, Max.

MAX

Did you know I have to sleep with the lights on?

(Rudy stares at him for a moment.)

RUDY

At least now you can put all this aside once and for all.

MAX

Rudy, I'm more determined than ever.

RUDY

What?

MAX

If people are this desperate to stop me, they must know I'm right. One day, there will be virtually no drugs. And I'll be the one to prove it's possible.

RUDY

Max, did it ever occur to you the opposite could be true? Perhaps these people are trying to stop you because you're thumbing your nose in the face of years of conventional wisdom?

MAX

I was up half the night rewriting the book. I'm starting from scratch. With my additional studies and the more patients I've healed, it's going to be even better than before. I'm keeping it under lock and key until it's finished. I know I can prove this, Rudy.

RUDY

In the face of everything you've been through?

MAX

(Looks at his watch) I must go. I'm off to Washington, D.C. in the morning.

RUDY

Washington?

MAX

I didn't tell you? I'm speaking before the Senate. There's an anti-cancer bill on the floor. They're asking for one hundred million dollars to fund alternative cancer therapies. Charlotte is going with me. I'm presenting five patients and reading case histories of five others. This is what I've been waiting for!

                    RUDY
                   (angry)
Max, you cannot do this!

                    MAX
Why, Rudy?

                    RUDY
Getting the government involved? You may start something you
can't stop.

                    MAX
I certainly hope so!

                    RUDY
Max. Listen to me. You don't know what you're dealing with.

                    MAX
But I do, Rudy. That's why I can't stop.

          (Max winces and grabs his stomach.)

                    RUDY
What's the matter?

                    MAX
It's nothing. A bit of gas.

                    RUDY
This is giving you an ulcer.

                    MAX
I'm alright. Once this bill passes and I get my funding, it will change
everything.

SCENE TWELVE.

> *(Crossfade to Heller's office as he crosses into the scene. Carmichael stands facing him.)*

RUDY
I did everything I could. So did Helga.

CARMICHAEL
I'm sure you did, Doc. It's not your fault she fell in love with him.

RUDY
Nothing ever happened between them.

CARMICHAEL
No? This looks like more than a friendly peck on the cheek to me.

> *(Carmichael reaches into his briefcase and hands Rudy a photograph.)*

CARMICHAEL (cont'd)
Right in your neighborhood, too. Some girls don't have any shame.

RUDY
It doesn't matter now. She's gone.

CARMICHAEL
Too bad. Good cousins are so hard to come by these days. So, any other thoughts about how to solve the Gerson problem?

RUDY
Not really.

CARMICHAEL
You know, the president of the AMA is stepping down. Dr. Fishbein got caught on a racketeering charge.

RUDY
I heard.

CARMICHAEL

Suppose you had the inside track?

RUDY

How could I possibly...?

(*Carmichael smiles at Rudy. Long pause.*)

RUDY (cont'd)

You bastard! He and I have been friends for years!

CARMICHAEL

Did I say a word?

RUDY

You didn't have to.

CARMICHAEL

That's because you know the answer as well as I do! Max Gerson is making you the butt of every joke in town...and I don't like seeing you laughed at. *(Sarcastically)* The body can heal itself! Curing diseases with nutrition! Smoking causes lung cancer! Jesus, if he were anyplace other than New York, he would have been lynched by now. A lot of people would think you were performing a public service. *(Pause.)* I've got something for you.

RUDY

What?

CARMICHAEL

A little gift from the Riser Pharmaceutical Company. Look out the window.

RUDY

I don't see anyth—

(Something catches Rudy's eye. He stops dead in his tracks.)

CARMICHAEL

A shiny, new red Packard. An important man like you shouldn't be taking the subway.

RUDY

I can't accept it.

CARMICHAEL

Why not?

RUDY

It's too much.

CARMICHAEL

Consider it a bonus.

(He puts the car keys on the table.)

CARMICHAEL (cont'd)

I'll leave it for a few days. Take it for a little spin. Maybe a drive upstate. Check out the autumn foliage. You've earned it, Rudy...by doing the right thing.

SCENE THIRTEEN.

(Max stands in front of a microphone. A GAVEL is heard. The PATIENTS enter and stand behind Max on either side of him like a Greek chorus.)

SENATOR PEPPER (V.O.)
Would you state your name for the record, please?

MAX
My name is Dr. Max Gerson. I am a member of the AMA, Medical Society of New York State, and Medical Society of New York County.

SENATOR PEPPER (V.O.)
Dr. Gerson, would you please explain your treatment?

MAX
The dietetic treatment which has for many years been known as the "Gerson Diet" was developed first to relieve my own severe migraine condition. Then it was successfully applied to patients with allergic conditions such as asthma, as well as diseases of the intestinal tract, the liver and pancreas.

ALICE HIRSCH
My name is Alice Hirsch. I had an inoperable tumor inside my spinal cord. They said I would never walk again and my days were numbered.

GEORGE GRIMSON
I'm George Grimson. I had a brain tumor. Half of my face was paralyzed and my left eye was swollen shut.

MAX
The great number of ailments which responded to the treatment showed clearly that the human body lost part of its resistance and healing power. When that is restored through a plant based diet, the body heals itself.

ANNA HENDRICKS
My name is Anna Hendricks. I had stomach cancer. I couldn't eat and I had growths on my liver.

WALTER FLEMING

I'm Walter Fleming. I had cancer of the lymph system. I had four painful surgeries that almost killed me.

ALL PATIENTS

The doctors said nothing more could be done and they sent me home to die.

ALICE HIRSCH

Then I went to Doctor Gerson.

WALTER FLEMING

Doctor Gerson.

GEORGE GRIMSON

Max Gerson.

ANNA HENDRICKS

I juiced the equivalent of twenty pounds of organic produce every day.

GEORGE GRIMSON

I quit smoking and drinking.

ALICE HIRSCH

He gave me vitamins and liver injections.

ANNA HENDRICKS

After five months, the tumor was gone.

WALTER FLEMING

After nine months, I was dancing at my daughter's bat mitzvah.

GEORGE GRIMSON

I'm back at work as if nothing happened.

ALICE HIRSCH

I'm making pottery again.

ANNA HENDRICKS

The X-rays look as if I was never even sick.

SENATOR PEPPER (V.O.)

Gentlemen, I think this is one of the most encouraging expressions of intelligent democracy I have ever seen. In light of such overwhelming evidence, I urge you to vote in favor of this bill.

> *(A gavel sounds, followed by cheering and applause. Max basks in the glow of his success.)*

SCENE FOURTEEN.

> *(Crossfade to Rudy, in a spotlight.)*

RUDY

The Pepper-Neely Hearings, named for the two senators who introduced the bill, went on for three days. Once they were over, Senator Claude Pepper was so impressed with Max's testimony, he called a press conference for the following day. When the drug lobbyists heard about it, they invited every journalist in town to a cocktail party, with an open bar and all the roast beef sandwiches they could eat. I thought to myself, "Poor Max. They all think he's insane. No one wants to hear about his pathetic, so-called cure." Only one man, Raymond Gram Swing, the respected journalist from ABC Radio, went to Pepper's press conference. The next day, he devoted an entire broadcast to Max Gerson's cancer therapy. For days afterwards, the switchboards at ABC lit up like a Christmas tree. Everyone wanted information on this alternative cure for cancer.

(While the spot remains up on Rudy, lights up on Max stage right sitting at the café. A waitress enters.)

WAITRESS

Hello, Doctor Gerson.

MAX

Hello, Esther. How's your brother getting along these days?

WAITRESS

A bit better, thanks to you. I'm afraid we don't have enough coffee left for your special brew but can I bring you something else?

MAX

Special brew?

WAITRESS

The coffee Dr. Heller brings.

MAX

But that was just the one time.

WAITRESS

He always brings in special coffee for you. I have strict orders not to serve it to anyone else.

MAX

Would you bring me the bag and what's left in it?

WAITRESS

Of course.

(As the waitress exits, Rudy, who has been watching the scene from the other side of the stage, addresses the audience.)

RUDY

In the last century, there was a pigment used by painters called Paris Green. Monet, Renoir and Cezanne all worked with it. Highly toxic. It might have been the reason Van Gogh cut off his ear. Elizabethan women used traces of this same element as face powder, mixed with vinegar and chalk. It gave them the lovely, pale complexion of noblewomen, not realizing what they were ingesting into their skin. At least no one could mistake them for a field hand when they expired.

(The waitress re-enters and hands Max the coffee bag. He takes a pinch of it, smells it then brings it to his lips.)

RUDY (cont'd)

In olden days, this same element was used to treat syphilis. Even cancer. It's tasteless and odorless and has the chemical symbol "As". As. To the same degree or amount. As bees to honey, as a knife through butter, as life to death. Arsenic. The poison of kings. In the coffee. For months. Lightly at first, just enough to slow him down. Now, with a vengeance. He's laughing at me! He's making a mockery of everything I hold sacred. If the Pepper-Neely Bill passes and he gets his funding, I'll be destroyed! So will hundreds of others. How can I let that happen? I saved his life once. I have every right to take it away.

SCENE FIFTEEN.

(Max walks quickly along a New York street, coughing heavily. Once again sees the doctor/Camel ad. This time, the doctor's face is an eerie skeleton. As he studies the ad, Max screams in terror. The traffic noises seem to grow louder in his head, combined with demonic laughter.)

MAX

Taxi! Taxi!

(Max starts to check his pulse and collapses. Charlotte enters and runs to him.)

                    CHARLOTTE
Vati!

                    (Charlotte lifts Max and helps him offstage.)

SCENE SIXTEEN.

                    (Crossfade to Max's bedroom. Charlotte
                    helps Max onto the bed, removes his shoes
                    and covers him.)

                    CHARLOTTE
You should have an X-Ray.

                    MAX
It's stress. The delay on the bill. I thought we'd have funding by now.

                    CHARLOTTE
What about a loan?

                    MAX
There's nothing left to borrow against.

                    CHARLOTTE
What about asking Rudy? Money seems to be the only thing he's good for.

                    MAX
He saved your life once.

                    CHARLOTTE
I still don't trust him.

118

MAX

But you'll take his money?

CHARLOTTE

Yes, if it would heal more patients.

> *(Max starts coughing deeply. He stops abruptly.)*

MAX

Did you hear that?

CHARLOTTE

What?

MAX

They're coming for me!

CHARLOTTE

Shh, *Vati.* It's the children playing kickball in the street. I'm admitting you to the hospital.

MAX

I won't go.

CHARLOTTE

Then, what about the therapy? The juicing, the coffee enemas--

MAX

It's too late for that.

CHARLOTTE

If one of your patients was this stubborn, you'd kick them to the curb.

MAX

Charlotte, promise me you'll keep the practice going.

CHARLOTTE

Of course, Vati, but--

MAX

And the research. You must find a way.

CHARLOTTE

I will, but--

MAX

Promise me!

CHARLOTTE

I promise. *(Sweetly)* You silly, old man. Now get some rest.

SCENE SEVENTEEN.

(Spotlight up on Rudy downstage.)

RUDY

I'm one of the richest doctors in America now. I travel all over the
world speaking about experimental cancer treatments - which ones
work, which don't. I have the full support of The American Medical
Association, The American Cancer Society and, of course, the Riser
Pharmaceutical Company. I always travel first class, stay in the best
hotels and I'm provided with anything I ask for.

CALL-GIRL
(Offstage)

Rudy! I'm waiting! *(Giggles)*

RUDY

I have a penthouse on Park Avenue, a dog, a housekeeper, the
newest cars and suits. This is the American dream! So, why am I

120

still plagued by him? Finally, Max got his answer. There were four United Sates senators who were former doctors. They had done everything in their power to crush the Pepper-Neely Bill. Two weeks after the broadcast, after thirty years with ABC News, Raymond Gram Swing was let go. The pharmaceutical companies threatened to cancel the advertising of every over-the-counter drug, which would have resulted in tens of thousands of dollars in losses for the network, if he wasn't fired. The Pepper-Neely bill was buried in bureaucratic red tape and never came up for a vote. And Max Gerson's testimony? The fine words from all of his healed patients? Completely expunged. Stricken from the record, never to be seen again.

SCENE EIGHTEEN.

>   *(Lights up on a bed and a chair downstage.*
>   *Charlotte applies a cloth to Max's head, as he*
>   *lies there, coughing and sputtering.)*

MAX

I wish I could have made it back to Hamburg. Better to die at home.

CHARLOTTE

Hush, Vati. You're too sick to travel. This is your home now.

(Rudy enters.)

RUDY

Hello, Max.

MAX

Is that you, my friend? Come closer.

RUDY

Hello, Charlotte.

CHARLOTTE
(coolly)

Rudy.

MAX

<u>Uncle</u> Rudy. Leave us for a moment.

CHARLOTTE

Call me if you need anything.

> *(Charlotte exits. Rudy sits in the chair next to the bed.)*

RUDY

Is there anything I can do?

MAX

Just sit with me for a moment. I want to imagine that we're back on the banks of the Elbe watching the sun set as we're studying for our exams. You're wearing your blue cap and I'm wearing my favorite sweater. The one with the patches on the elbows.

RUDY
(fondly)

I always hated that sweater. You looked like you were wearing a potato sack.

MAX

You never told me! My mother knitted it for my sixteenth birthday.

RUDY
(smiling)

That's why I never told you.

> *(Max tries to laugh and coughs.)*

MAX

Anything else you never told me?

(Rudy shakes his head 'No".)

MAX (cont'd)

Are you sure?

(Rudy hesitates then nods.)

MAX (cont'd)

It doesn't matter. I forgive you, anyway. *(Pause.)* Remember Otka? The ugly waitress?

RUDY

Of course.

MAX

I took her to bed once. Out of pity.

RUDY
(laughing)

You dog!

MAX

It was terrible. The worst "schtup" I ever had!

RUDY

I hope she enjoyed it, at least.

MAX

I know you never approved of my natural healing. I didn't mean to embarrass you. I only did what I felt I had to.

RUDY

Shh. You mustn't strain yourself.

MAX

I've finished the book. *A Cancer Therapy* will be published in the Spring.

RUDY
(flatly)

Congratulations, Max.

MAX

So much better than before. Helga actually did me a favor. *(A twinkle in his eye.)* Despite everything, I think she liked me.

RUDY

I'm sure she did. *(Pause.)* I've written a check. To help with some of your debts.

MAX

I can't let you do that.

RUDY

It's already done.

MAX

Charlotte will be so relieved. Keep an eye on her, Rudy.

RUDY

If she'll let me.

MAX

She's stubborn. Like me. But she needs looking after.

RUDY

I'll do my best.

(Max's breathing gets more labored.)

MAX

I have to sleep now.

RUDY

I'll stop by tomorrow. Good night.

MAX

Goodbye, my friend.

(Max takes Rudy's hand and holds it tightly.
Rudy smiles at him, then looks away. Finally,
Max lets go of his hand. Rudy crosses
downstage to the corner of his living room
seen at the top of the play.)

SCENE NINETEEN.

RUDY
(to audience)
That was the last time I saw Max Gerson alive. What did he mean he
"forgave me anyway"? The death certificate said "lung cancer".
They never did an autopsy, so no one knew about the massive holes
in his lungs caused by the ingestion of arsenic. "*Finita la*
Commedia"

(Lights up on the other side of the stage on a middle-aged Charlotte
Gerson, who is greeted by a smattering of applause. She speaks
warmly.)

CHARLOTTE

Thank you for coming today. It is with great pleasure that I welcome
you to the twenty-fifth anniversary celebration of the Gerson
Institute. I am Charlotte Gerson. My father was a pioneer in the
world of natural healing long before it was fashionable or even
accepted. To date, the Gerson therapy has cured over ten thousand
people of terminal illnesses. Imagine how much higher that number
might have been if we'd had the support of the established medical
community?

(On the other side of the stage, the telephone
rings. Rudy answers it.)

125

RUDY

Yes?

(Spot up on Carmichael.)

CARMICHAEL

Congratulations, Rudy!

RUDY
(unemotionally)

Thank you.

CHARLOTTE

While the Gerson method is accepted as an alternative cancer therapy throughout Europe and Asia, it is still illegal in most of the United States to treat cancer with anything other than surgery, radiation and chemotherapy. Since a doctor could lose his license for practicing what my father proved more than fifty years ago, I work with clinics in Tijuana and Budapest. In other countries, it is not considered a criminal offense to heal someone by altering their diet.

CARMICHAEL

You don't sound very excited.

RUDY

I suppose I'm in shock.

CHARLOTTE

Even today, roughly ninety per cent of all oncologists see no connection whatsoever between cancer and nutrition. Perhaps that's because they have so little training in it. What most doctors don't tell you is that chemotherapy is so toxic, it can actually cause cancer. Since the 1950's, more people have been killed by its negative effects than were killed by Hitler and Stalin combined. And the success rate for healing from chemotherapy and radiation is so incredibly low, if it weren't for the billions of dollars in revenue it generates every year, it would be categorized as a placebo. No better

than a sugar pill. But there is very little money to be made in
treating cancer with fruits and vegetables.

CARMICHAEL

Well, of course you're in shock. Now, I'll see you at 8 o'clock in
your tux. We're going to celebrate.

RUDY

Meet me here. I'll leave the door unlocked.

CARMICHAEL

Anything you say, Doc. I've got a table at The Stork Club and a
couple of the hottest little fillies you've ever seen. Either one of 'em
could curl your toes faster than you can say "Max Gerson". By the
way, I saw his obit in the paper today. That must be tough for you.

RUDY

You have no idea.

CARMICHAEL
(singing)
"Forget your troubles, C'mon get happy..." Rudolph Heller -
President of the American Medical Association! We did it! I'll see
you tonight.

> *(Rudy hangs up the phone. The light goes out
> on Carmichael.)*

> *(The Woman in the Coat from the opening
> scene enters and sits by herself, isolated in a
> spot.)*

CHARLOTTE

In spite of all the so-called advances in research, roughly 20,000
people die of cancer every day. This translates to 8 million deaths a
year. More than half a million are Americans. Treating this disease
remains one of the biggest businesses in America, generating over
115 billion dollars every year. It is estimated that by the year 2020,
more than half of the cases of cancer in America will be medically

induced by drugs or radiation. That means the American medical establishment itself will be the leading cause of cancer.

> *(Rudy switches on the hi-fi. "Get Happy" plays. He reaches into the desk drawer and pulls out a revolver. The record starts skipping, playing the same phrase - "Judgement day" - over and over again. Rudy cocks the revolver and places it in his mouth. Blackout on Rudy.)*

CHARLOTTE (cont'd)
(smiling - with no bitterness)
People will tell you I'm crazy. They'll say my father was a quack. Many people tried to stop him. If I hadn't carried on his legacy, they might have succeeded. Scientists will tell you there is no hard proof that the body can heal itself. But let me ask you this. Go visit a cancer patient's support group sometime. See if there is one, lonely, but determined woman sitting by herself in the corner. She has been coming to these meetings for more than three years and she has watched all of her friends die. When you ask her what she's done differently from all the others, she tells you that she stopped taking drugs and switched to a plant based diet. This has made it possible for her to watch her youngest son get married next month. What other proof does one need?

> *(The light slowly fades out on Charlotte and remains on the Woman in the Coat, who rises.)*

WOMAN
My name is Helga. And I am a cancer survivor.

> *(The light on the Woman gets brighter and brighter before it slowly fades.)*

THE END

About the Playwright

Luke Yankee (yes, it's his real name) is a writer, director, producer, actor and teacher. He is the author of the memoir, *Just Outside the Spotlight: Growing Up with Eileen Heckart* (published by Random House, with a foreword by Mary Tyler Moore). Renowned performing arts critic Michael Musto placed it on his list of the Ten Best Celebrity Memoirs and called it "One of the most compassionate, illuminating showbiz books ever written."

His play, *The Last Lifeboat* (dealing with the aftermath of the sinking of The Titanic) is published by Dramatists Play Service and has had more than 20 productions in North America. The Canadian production won twelve awards at two different theatre festivals in British Columbia. He developed the screenplay of *The Last Lifeboat* at the DreamAgo screenwriters workshop in the Swiss Alps, where he was one of ten writers chosen internationally.

His numerous, award-winning screenplays, spec scripts and television pilots include *The Lavender Mafia* (about the emergence of the gay "power elite" in 1950's Hollywood) which is currently being shopped to producers.

His play, *The Jesus Hickey* is the winner of the TRU Voices Award, as well as the Joel and Phyllis Ehrlich Award, given for "a socially relevant, commercially viable, new work of theatre." He directed the Los Angeles premiere at the Skylight Theatre, starring Harry Hamlin. The published version and eBook is available through Amazon.

Luke's first play, *A Place at Forest Lawn* (also published by Dramatists Play Service) has been produced at several regional theatres around the country. It is the recipient of the New Noises Award as well as the Palm Springs International Playwriting Festival. It was developed in workshops in New York and Los Angeles featuring Betty White, Marion Ross, Tony Goldwyn, Marcia Cross, Barbara Rush, Pat Carroll, Frances Sternhagen, John Glover and Millicent Martin.

Luke has served as the Producing Artistic Director of the Long Beach Civic Light Opera (one of the largest musical theatres in America) and the Struthers Library Theatre (an historic opera house in Northwestern Pennsylvania). He has assistant directed six Broadway plays, including *The Circle* starring Sir Rex Harrison, *Light Up the Sky* with Peter Falk, *Grind* starring Ben Vereen (directed by Harold Prince) and has directed and produced Off-Broadway and at regional theatres throughout the country and abroad.

He has taught and guest directed extensively at colleges, universities and conservatories throughout the U.S. and abroad. He holds his MFA in Writing for the Performing Arts from the University of California, Riverside and a BA from New York University. Luke also studied acting at the Juilliard School of Drama, Circle in the Square and Northwestern.

His website is www.lukeyankee.com.

For more books and DVDs on Dr. Max Gerson and The Gerson Therapy, go to www.gersonmedia.com.

Made in the USA
San Bernardino, CA
07 July 2017